An Elephant Came to Swim

Hugh Lewin and Lisa Kopper

Hamish Hamilton · London

"We have a problem," Sekuru said. "Here we have this lovely hotel on the hill, just off the main road, with plenty of comfortable rooms, a beautiful view across the valley, and a large verandah overlooking a swimming pool. But nobody comes to stay. We have asked our friends to tell everyone about our hotel. We have a dance every Saturday night and a feast on Sundays, but there are so few customers we may have to close down."

"What about the dogs? And the chickens and cats? And the cow and the duck and the monkey?" the children asked. "This is their home too."
"But they don't pay for their keep," said Sekuru. "How can I feed everyone if no guests pay to stay in the hotel? I'll have to go to town tomorrow to borrow money."

But early next morning his shouts brought everyone from their beds. There, walking up the drive as if he owned the place, was the biggest, tuskiest elephant they had ever seen. His ears were flapping. His trunk was swishing. He strolled up to the front door and tried to open it.

Then he humphed off across the lawn and walked straight into the swimming pool. He drew gallons of water into his trunk and sloshed it all over himself, across his back, behind his ears, and up at his tummy. Then he rolled over and over soaking himself. The dogs barked. Shoko the monkey chattered across the roof. The chickens scattered, and Dadha the duck waddled towards the pool, her tail flip-flapping, to meet the intruder.

The elephant stood still, watching her.
"Quack," she said loudly. Dadha stretched her
head forward. "Quack," she said again, and
made as if to step into the pool.

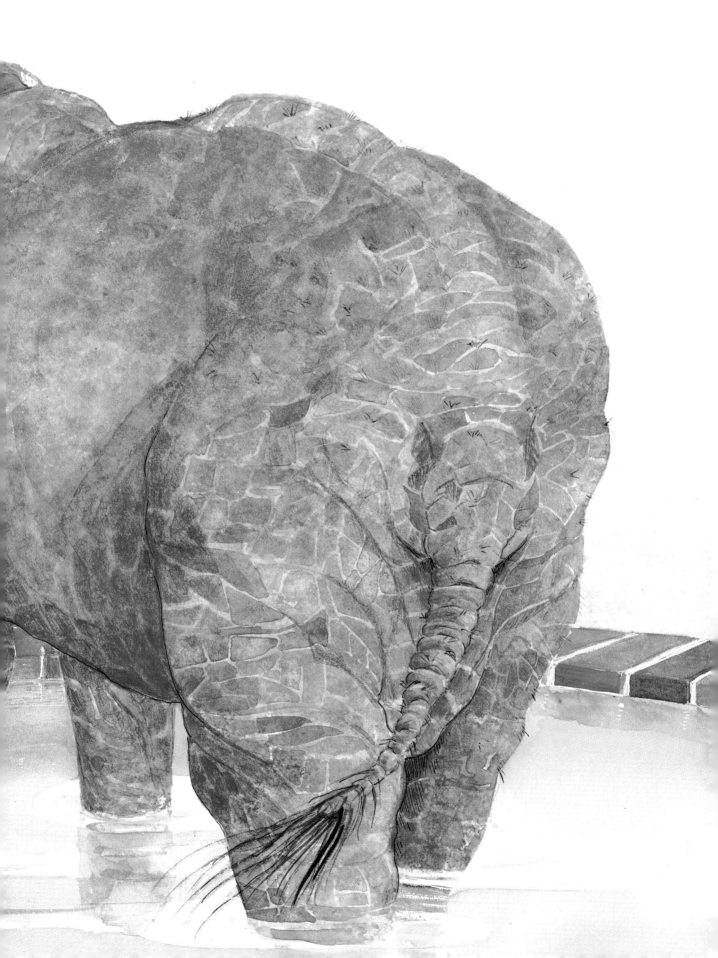

Suddenly the elephant lifted his trunk and shot
a burst of water at poor Dadha, knocking her
back onto the lawn, her feet flapping at the
sky.

Dadha stomped off in disgust as the elephant bowed to the cheers from the verandah.
"Hooray, Mister Ellie," they shouted.
"Let's have breakfast," said Sekuru. So they all sat down on the verandah and watched Mister Ellie playing in the water.

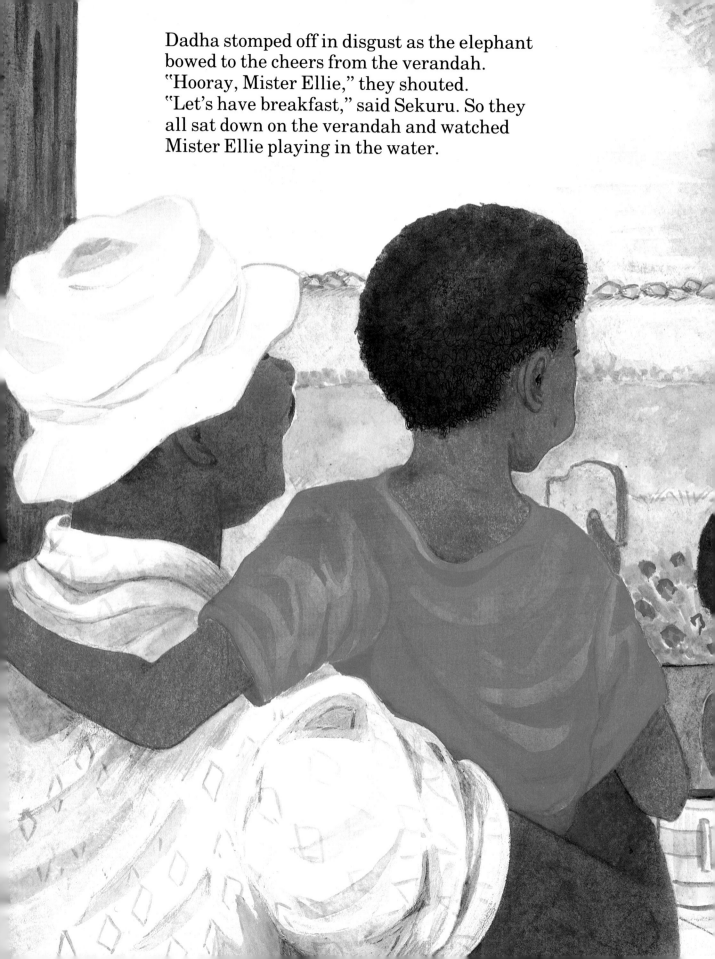

"What's he doing in the pool?" asked the people from the village when they arrived after breakfast.
"Will he bring his family?" asked Sekuru's friends who came soon afterwards.
"Has he come to stay?" asked the travellers who stopped their cars when they saw the crowd on the verandah.

As each new group arrived, Mister Ellie lifted
his trunk and gave a trumpet of welcome.
"We are the animals now," said Sekuru. "He's
watching us."

There was a great deal for Mister Ellie to watch as more and more cars arrived and the waiters scurried back and forth with trays of drinks for each new group of guests. Soon the verandah was full, the lounge was full, the windows of the rooms were full, and some of the children climbed the trees. Everyone was watching Mister Ellie.

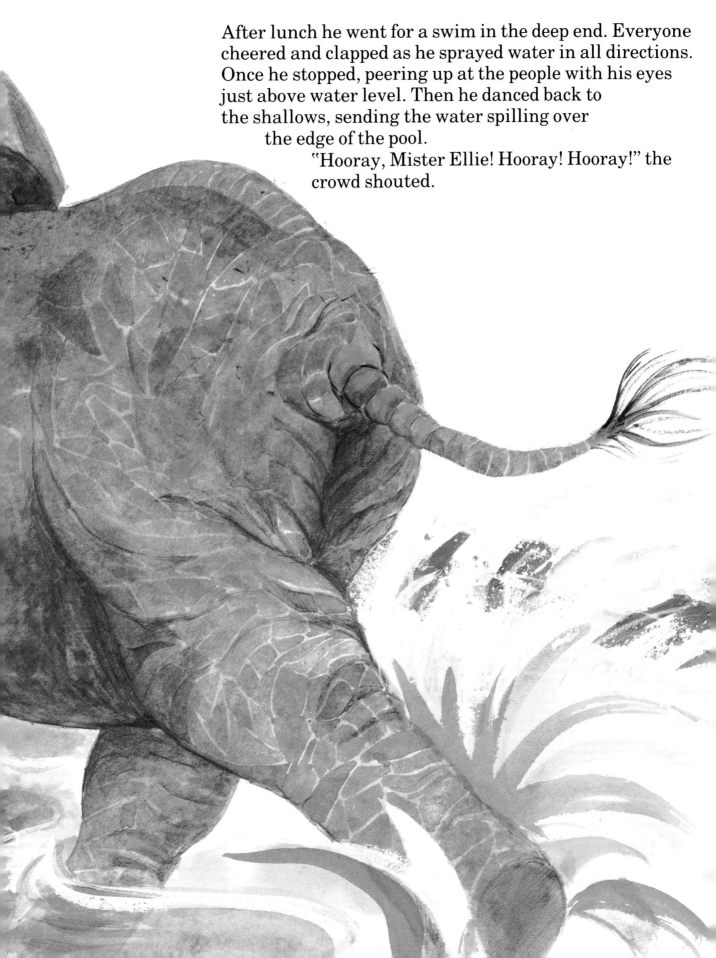

After lunch he went for a swim in the deep end. Everyone cheered and clapped as he sprayed water in all directions. Once he stopped, peering up at the people with his eyes just above water level. Then he danced back to the shallows, sending the water spilling over the edge of the pool.

"Hooray, Mister Ellie! Hooray! Hooray!" the crowd shouted.

Then, as the sun dipped red behind the hill, Mister Ellie shook himself and climbed out of the pool. He waved his trunk before walking off down the drive and into the trees beyond the main road, leaving behind the excited crowd and the waves lapping gently in the empty pool.

"It's time for a celebration," said Sekuru, and he ordered drinks for everyone.

So when next you stop at the friendly hotel on the hill, as so many people do now, Sekuru will be sure to tell you of the day when the elephant came to swim in the pool and saved the hotel from closing down. Don't forget to take an extra bun . . . just in case Mister Ellie decides to visit again.

First published 1985
Published by Hamish Hamilton Children's Books
Garden House   57–59 Long Acre   London WC2E 9JZ
Copyright (text) © 1985 Hugh Lewin
Copyright (illustrations) © 1985 Lisa Kopper

British Library in Cataloguing in Publication Data
Lewin, Hugh
An elephant came to swim
I. Title
823,.914   [J]   PZ7

ISBN 0-241-11432-2

Typeset by Katerprint Co. Ltd, Oxford

Printed in Great Britain by
Cambus Litho, East Kilbride